DINK, JOSH, AND RUTH ROSE
AREN'T THE ONLY KID DETECTIVES!

WHAT ABOUT YOU?

CAN YOU FIND THE HIDDEN MESSAGE INSIDE THIS BOOK?

There are 26 illustrations in this book, not counting the one on the title page, the map at the beginning, and the picture of the valentines that repeats at the start of many of the chapters. In each of the 26 illustrations, there's a hidden letter. If you can find all the letters, you will spell out a secret message!

If you're stumped, the answer is on the bottom of page 129.

HAPPY DETECTING!

This book is dedicated to
Kayden Myrick, whom I admire openly.
—R.R.

To Secret Admirers everywhere!
—J.S.G.

Text copyright © 2015 by Ron Roy
Cover art copyright © 2015 by Stephen Gilpin
Interior illustrations copyright © 2015 by John Steven Gurney

Visit us on the Web!
SteppingStonesBooks.com
randomhousekids.com

Educators and librarians, for a variety of teaching tools,
visit us at RHTeachersLibrarians.com

Library of Congress Cataloging-in-Publication Data is available upon request.
ISBN 978-0-553-52399-7 (trade) — ISBN 978-0-553-52400-0 (lib. bdg.) —
ISBN 978-0-553-52401-7 (ebook)

Printed in the United States of America
10 9 8 7 6 5 4 3 2

This book has been officially leveled by using the F&P Text Level Gradient™ Leveling System.

A to Z Mysteries®

SUPER EDITION 8

Secret Admirer

by **Ron Roy**

illustrated by
John Steven Gurney

A STEPPING STONE BOOK™

Random House New York

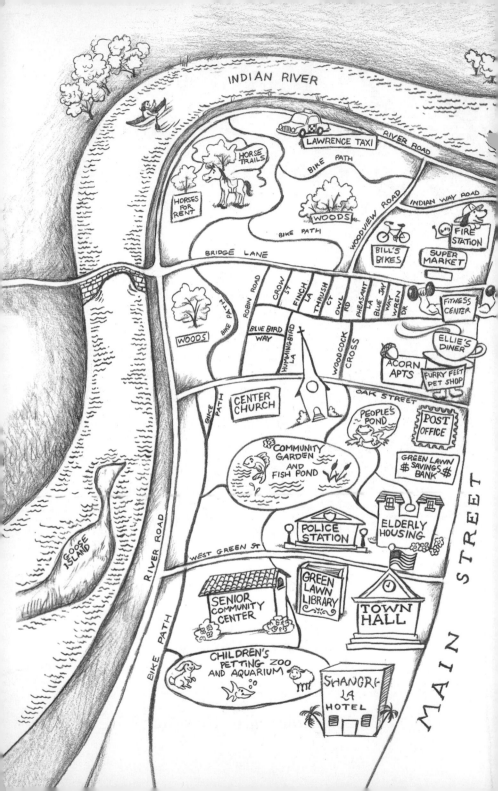

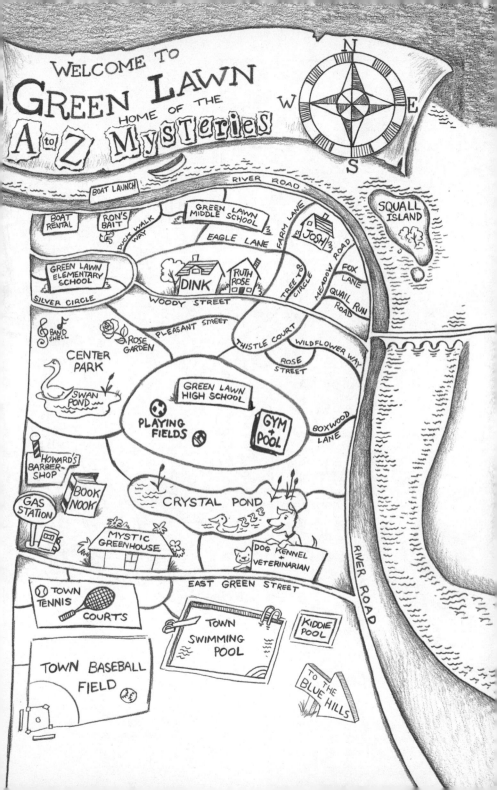

CHAPTER 1

"I hate being in fourth grade," Josh said. He tossed a squishy football to Dink. It was Saturday afternoon, and snowing. Dink, Josh, and Ruth Rose were hanging out at Josh's house, upstairs in his room.

"Why?" Dink asked. "Don't you think it's cool being one of the older kids at school?" He chucked the ball to Ruth Rose.

She caught the ball and flipped it over to Josh. "I love being almost ten!" Ruth Rose said. "Finally, I'll have two numbers in my age!"

Josh sighed and got off his bed. He motioned for Dink and Ruth Rose to follow him. He tiptoed in his socks out into the hall, and they did, too. He stopped in front of Bradley and Brian's bedroom door. Dink and Ruth Rose were right behind him.

"Listen," Josh whispered.

This is what they heard:

"I can hardly wait to get to school on Monday!" Bradley said.

"Me too," Brian said. "It'll be Valentine's Day!"

"We're getting a cupcake party and a Valentine's box and a movie and show-and-tell!" Nate added. Nate was Ruth Rose's little brother and Bradley and Brian's best friend.

"Come on," Josh whispered. He walked to his parents' bedroom door and stopped.

His mom was sitting at her desk,

chatting away on her cell phone.

This is what the kids heard:

"I found my husband the cutest Valentine's Day present!" she said. "And I'm cooking his favorite dinner. I know he's gotten me something nice, too. He says he forgot all about Valentine's Day, but I know he's just teasing me!"

Josh sighed and staggered back to his bedroom with Dink and Ruth Rose behind him.

"It's not fair," Josh moaned, throwing himself on his bed. Dink and Ruth Rose sat on the floor. Pal wandered in, leaped onto the bed, and licked Josh's chin.

"Maybe we'll get cupcakes at school Monday," Ruth Rose offered. "Or something."

"It'll never happen," Dink said. "Josh is right. Only the little kids get parties on Valentine's Day."

Josh closed his eyes. "You know what we get? Nothing!"

He sighed again.

Dink sighed.

Ruth Rose sighed.

Pal sighed as Josh stroked his long, silky ears.

The next morning was Sunday. Dink carried Loretta's cage downstairs to the kitchen. He liked to clean it every weekend. He set it on the counter, then ran back upstairs and grabbed a bag of pine chips.

Dink and Loretta had a routine: Dink placed the guinea pig on the floor. She sniffed for crumbs under the kitchen table while he washed the inside of the cage. Then he spread clean pine chips on the bottom.

Before Dink could fill Loretta's little dishes with fresh water and food, the doorbell rang.

"Who's here so early?" his mother asked as she walked into the kitchen.

"Watch out for Loretta, Mom," Dink said. "She's under the table."

"I see her," his mom said. "Good morning, Loretta!" Then she opened the door.

Dink's two best friends stood on the doorstep. "Good morning, Josh and Ruth Rose!" Dink's mom said. "Come on in."

"Hi, Mrs. Duncan!" Josh and Ruth Rose said. They came in and hung up their jackets and kicked out of their boots.

"I like your outfit!" Dink's mother told Ruth Rose.

Ruth Rose liked to dress in a different color each day. Today she wore a green sweater, green jeans, and a green headband.

Josh had on a thick white sweater and cargo pants.

"Josh, what're those brown hairs all over your sweater?" Dink's mother asked.

Josh looked down at his chest. "Oh, I was brushing Polly," he said. "Her coat gets all shaggy in the winter. She loves it when I use a stiff brush to groom her."

"She loved it all over your sweater," Ruth Rose said.

"Yeah," Josh said. "While I'm brushing her, she gives me pony kisses."

Dink's mother smiled. "What are pony kisses?" she asked.

"Polly rubs her lips on my ear," Josh said. "It feels like two warm marshmallows!"

"Hey, guys," Dink called. "What's going on?"

"We came to get you to come out and play in the snow," Josh said.

"And we found this on your doormat!" Ruth Rose handed Dink a little white lump, wrapped in clear tape. "I think it's a note!"

Dink turned the taped note over in his hands. It felt cold and damp.

"Come into the kitchen, you two,"

Dink's mother said. "Have you eaten breakfast?"

"I did," Ruth Rose said.

"Me too," Josh said. "But I could always eat another piece of chocolate cake!"

Dink's mother laughed. "How about a piece of toast?" she asked.

Josh beamed. "With peanut butter?"

"Of course," she said. "Chunky, your favorite."

Josh and Ruth Rose followed Dink into the kitchen.

"Watch where you step," Dink told his friends. "Loretta's on the floor."

Dink sat at the table and picked at the taped note with his fingernail. When that didn't work, he took scissors from a drawer.

Josh flopped on the floor and reached for Loretta. He sat her on his chest and petted her soft fur. Loretta made cute little squeaky noises.

"Loretta loves me!" Josh said. "She just said so!"

Ruth Rose laughed. "I think Loretta *loves* Dink," she said. "She only *likes* you, Josh."

Josh tickled Loretta's tummy. She squeaked again.

"Here's the bread and the toaster," Dink's mother said. "The peanut butter is on the table, and pour yourselves some juice."

Josh put Loretta into her cage, then dropped a slice of bread into a toaster slot. Ruth Rose poured two glasses of orange juice.

Dink finally removed the tape. Inside was a white paper, folded four times. He flattened the paper on the table and read six words: WHERE DOES ABE LINCOLN HANG OUT?

"What does it say?" Josh asked, spreading peanut butter on his toast.

"It's a weird note," Dink said. He handed the message to Josh.

"Where does Abe Lincoln hang out?" Josh read. "I don't get it."

Mrs. Duncan was looking over Dink's shoulder. She glanced at a calendar hanging on the wall. "Maybe it has something to do with Lincoln's birthday. That was yesterday, February twelfth."

Josh dropped the note and took a big bite of his toast.

Ruth Rose read the message as she sipped her juice. "It looks like some kind of mystery clue," she said.

"Well, Abe used to hang out in his log cabin," Dink said after a minute. "He hung out at the White House, too, when he was president."

His mom shook her head. "Those were in the past," she said. "I think your note asks where he hangs out *now*. It asks, where *does* he hang out?"

"Now?" Dink said. "How could President Lincoln hang out anywhere? He's dead!"

"So he hangs out in his tomb," Josh said.

Dink studied the note again. "Oh, I know! He hangs out on money!"

"His face is on five-dollar bills," Ruth Rose said.

Dink looked at his mother's purse, sitting on the counter. "Do you have any fives, Mom?"

"I might." She opened her purse and took out her wallet. She emptied a few bills and coins onto the table. "Yep, here's one." She handed a five-dollar bill to Dink.

Josh and Ruth Rose stood behind Dink, and they looked at Abe Lincoln's picture on the bill. He had shaggy hair, deep lines near his mouth, and wrinkles around his eyes. "Why does he look so sad?" Dink asked.

"I think our sixteenth president was a sad man," his mom said. "The Civil War made him unhappy. He was depressed because all those fighting men were being killed. And two of his sons got sick and died. Two little boys."

Josh looked up. "President Lincoln had sons who died?" he said. "I didn't know that. How old were they?"

"Well, if I remember my history correctly, Eddie was President Lincoln's second son. He died when he was only three years old," Dink's mother said. "That was before Mr. Lincoln became president, and before the Civil War. Then, twelve years later, his third son, Willie, got sick. He died in 1862, the week after the president's birthday and Valentine's Day. It was a very sad February in the White House."

Dink looked at Lincoln's sad face, and thought about the president losing his sons at such an early age.

His mother pushed the coins toward him. "Put these in your money jug," she said. Then she grinned. "I hope you can save enough for your college education!"

Dink grinned right back at her. "Can I put the five-dollar bill in my jug, too?" he asked.

His mom snatched the bill from Dink's fingers. "Nope, that goes back in my wallet, kiddo!"

"Thanks, Mom," Dink said. He put the coins in his pocket.

"Boy, you're lucky," Josh said. "I have to work to get money!"

"I do, too," Dink said, picking up Loretta's cage. Josh and Ruth Rose quickly cleared the table, then followed Dink to his room. Dink set the cage on his desk.

In one corner of his bedroom stood a big glass jug half-filled with pennies, nickels, dimes, and quarters. Dink dropped the new coins in.

"You'll need a lot more to pay for college," Josh said.

Looking at all those coins, Dink suddenly realized something. "Guys, Abraham Lincoln's face is on pennies, too!" he said.

Dink reached into the jug, took out some coins, and dropped them on his bed. He chose a penny and peered at Lincoln's face. On the penny, President Lincoln was looking off to one side. "He looks sad on the penny, too," Dink said.

Josh picked up some coins. Thomas Jefferson's face was on the nickel, and he didn't look happy, either. President Franklin Roosevelt was on the dime. No smile there, either. George Washington looked unhappy on the quarter.

"It's hard work being a president," Ruth Rose said. "But I still want the job when I'm old enough."

"I'll vote for you!" Josh said. "It'll be so cool to visit you in the White House!"

Dink returned the coins to the jug. He didn't know why someone had left that silly note on his front steps. *Where does Abe Lincoln hang out?*

As Dink was shoving the jug back into the corner, Josh grabbed his arm. "Wait, what's that under the jug?" he asked Dink.

The three kids tipped it on its side. Something square and red was taped to the bottom.

"It's a Valentine's card!" Ruth Rose said.

CHAPTER 2

Dink pulled the card off and stood the jug back up. Someone had written *Dink* in yellow glitter on the front of the envelope.

"Open it!" Josh said. He and Ruth Rose were right behind Dink.

"I will if you chill," Dink told Josh. He flipped the envelope over. It was sealed with tape—the same kind of tape that had been wrapped around the note downstairs.

Dink opened the envelope and slid out a card. On the front was a picture of a big red heart, covered with more glitter. Below the heart he saw two small pictures, a number 4, and some letters.

Dink blinked in confusion. "This doesn't make any sense," he muttered. He laid the card on his desk so Josh and Ruth Rose could see it.

The first picture was a drawing of a human eye with eyelashes. The second picture looked like a slice of pie. After that came the letter *N*, the number 4, and the letter *U*.

The kids had seen word puzzles like this before. Whoever made up the puzzles used pictures instead of words.

"*4 U* probably means *for you*," Ruth Rose said. "And this eye could stand for the letter *I*."

"And the next picture is a piece of blueberry pie!" Josh said.

Dink stared at the mysterious message. *"I dessert for you?"* he mumbled.

"I blueberry for you?" He giggled.

His mother stuck her head into his room. "I'm going to the mall," she said. "I won't be long."

Dink held up the card. "Look what I found under my penny jug," he said.

"Oooh, a Valentine's card!" his mom said. "Who sent it?"

"I don't know, and I don't get the message on the card," Dink said.

His mom glanced at the card. "That says *I pine for you,*" she read.

"Pine? Like a pinecone or a pineapple?" Dink asked. "That's a piece of pie, Mom. How do you get *pine?*"

His mother put her finger on the letter *N* after the picture of the pie slice. "*Pie* plus the *N* is *pine,*" she said. "The message says *I pine for you.*"

Dink shook his head. "Cool, Mom. But what's that supposed to mean?"

She smiled. "If someone *pines* for you, it means they really, really like you!" she said, taking the card. "Oh goodness! Did you see what it says on the bottom? You have a secret admirer, honey!"

"I do not!" Dink said. He grabbed the card back as his mom laughed. He looked at words written near the bottom of the card: FROM YOUR SEKRET ADMIRER.

Josh and Ruth Rose read the words, too.

"Well, they spelled *secret* wrong," Josh said. "Who wants a secret admirer who can't even spell *secret*?"

"Well, good luck finding out who pines for you!" Dink's mother said as she left.

Josh grinned at Dink. "Someone liiiiikes you!" he teased.

Dink stared at Josh. "Did *you* leave the note and stick this card under my penny jar?" he demanded. "If you did, I'll . . ."

Josh shook his head. "Nope. Not me," he said. "Maybe it was Ruth Rose!"

"Ha!" Ruth Rose said. "I'm a good speller, Joshua!"

Dink stared out the window at the falling snowflakes. "Then who could it be?" he wondered out loud.

"Maybe your mom did it," Josh said.

"Goofing on you for Valentine's Day."

Dink shook his head. "She's an excellent speller, too," he said.

Ruth Rose studied the note on both sides. She examined the card, front and back. Finally, she picked up the envelope and peeked inside. "Aha!" she said. "There's something else in here!"

"What?" Dink asked.

Ruth Rose put two fingers into the bottom of the envelope and pulled out a piece of cardboard. It was two inches long and about one inch wide. The cardboard looked as if it had been cut from a cereal box top. On the blank side the kids read these words: *Where does a buddy snore?*

"Another crazy clue!" Dink said.

"Wait, there's more," Ruth Rose said. She held the envelope upside down and tapped it on the desk. Six tiny squares of paper fell out.

"What are these?" Josh asked. "They look like they were cut out of a comic book. See, there's Spider-Man's face."

"But on the other side, each one has a capital letter," Ruth Rose said. She lined them up on the desk. *P, E, S, E, L, S.*

The kids stared at the six letters.

"What do they mean?" Josh asked.

"Nothing," Dink said.

CHAPTER 3

Josh grabbed the piece of cardboard. *"Where does a buddy snore?"* he read. He waved it at Dink. "Who's Buddy?"

Dink took the message and laid it next to the one asking where Abe Lincoln hung out. "The writing looks different," he said, comparing the two.

"Dude, who's Buddy?" Josh asked again.

"I don't know anyone named Buddy," Dink said. "Besides, it says *a buddy,* not Buddy. The *B* isn't capitalized. Either way, I don't know."

"My brother has a stuffed giraffe," Ruth Rose said.

"My brothers have stuffed tigers," Josh said. "So . . . ?"

"Nate named his giraffe Gerard," Ruth Rose continued, "but he calls it his buddy. When he was little, he never asked, 'Where's Gerard?' He always said, 'Where's my buddy?'"

"So you think your brother sent me these notes?" Dink asked. He grinned. "Little Nate Hathaway is my secret admirer?"

"No, of course not," Ruth Rose said. "I'm just saying he calls his giraffe a buddy, like in your note."

Dink and Josh stared at her.

"Your first note asked you about Abe Lincoln, and you found this Valentine's card under your jug of Lincoln pennies," Ruth Rose went on. "So maybe we'll find another card under Nate's giraffe."

"You think *a buddy* in this note is your brother's buddy, the giraffe named Gerard?" Dink asked.

Ruth Rose shrugged. "I'm just saying," she said.

"We should go check it out," Josh said.

Dink put everything back into the envelope, folded it, and slipped it into his pocket.

The kids pulled on their boots and coats and ran next door to Ruth Rose's house. "MOM, I'M HOME!" she yelled.

"Take off your boots and stop yelling!" her mother yelled from the living room.

They pulled off their boots, and Ruth Rose led them up the stairs to Nate's bedroom.

"Looks like a bomb went off in here," Josh commented. Clothes and toys and sneakers and games were everywhere. "It's disgusting how messy some children are!"

Dink and Ruth Rose laughed. "We've seen *your* room," Dink said.

On a shelf over Nate's unmade bed, Dink saw a row of stuffed animals. In the middle of some pigs and bears and hippos sat a giraffe missing one eye. His long neck was bent, and his gangly legs hung over the edge of the shelf.

"Is that Gerard?" Dink asked.

"That's him," Ruth Rose said. "He sleeps on that shelf, with all of Nate's other little stuffed buddies."

"Does anyone see a red envelope?" Dink asked.

They searched Nate's room. They found red pajamas, a red book, and a red ball, but no red Valentine's Day card.

Ruth Rose stood on her brother's
bed and removed all the stuffed animals
from the shelf. She laid them on Nate's
pillow. "No card up here," she said,
sweeping her hand along the shelf.

"I guess we got the wrong buddy,"
Josh said.

While Ruth Rose replaced Nate's
stuffed animals, Dink pulled the envelope from his pocket. He read the message on the two-inch cardboard again.
Josh and Ruth Rose looked over Dink's
shoulder.

"I wonder why *buddy* is underlined," Dink said.

"Well, we already know this secret admirer can't spell *secret*," Josh said. "So maybe *buddy* isn't spelled right, either. What if whoever wrote it meant a *body,* not a *buddy*?"

"What kind of body?" Dink asked.

"A dead body!" Josh said.

Ruth Rose let out a laugh.

"Where does a body snore?" Josh whispered in a Halloween voice. "Hey, I know the answer! A dead body snores in a grave. We have to go to the cemetery and dig up a grave!"

Ruth Rose poked Dink. "I think *someone in this room* is watching too much television!" she whispered loud enough for Josh to hear her.

Ruth Rose grabbed Nate's *My First Dictionary* from his desk. She turned pages until she got to the *B*'s. "Listen to this," she said. "A buddy is *a friend, a comrade, or a pal.*"

"Cool," Josh said, "but that doesn't help."

Something clicked in Dink's brain. But he couldn't see it yet.

"We still have these letters," Dink said. "Maybe they'll help." He spilled the six little letters onto the page of Nate's dictionary.

"They must spell something," Ruth Rose said. She arranged the letters until they read *E, L, P, S, E, S.*

Josh said, "What the heck are *elpses*?"

Ruth Rose moved the letters again and got *P, L, E, E, S, S.* "It could be *pleess*," she read. "Is that a word?"

"If it's supposed to be *please*, it isn't spelled right," Josh said.

Dink held up the piece of cardboard. "*Buddy* is underlined, which must mean something," he said. "And it says *a buddy.* So maybe the secret admirer wanted us to think of another word that means the same as a buddy."

He picked up the six letters from the dictionary page and slipped them back into the envelope. Halfway down the page, he saw the word *buddy* and its meaning: *a friend, a comrade, or a pal.* Something clicked in his brain again. This time he saw a brown-and-white dog with long, floppy ears.

Dink glanced over at Josh. "We all know a dog named Pal, don't we?" he asked.

CHAPTER 4

"Oh my gosh!" Josh said. "Maybe *a buddy* means a pal—*my* Pal!"

Ruth Rose grinned at Josh. "Now we just have to find where Pal snores."

"Pal snores everywhere!" Josh said. "On my bed, on the couch, under the kitchen table, in the backyard. . . ."

"Well, let's go check out some of them!" Ruth Rose said.

Dink put the cardboard back into the envelope with the card and cutout letters, and returned the envelope to his pocket.

The kids pulled on their snow gear and headed out.

The snow came up to their ankles, and they left deep footprints as they hiked up Farm Lane from Woody Street. It was a cold, snowy Sunday, and they didn't see any cars as they crossed Eagle Lane. They couldn't even see

Josh's house until they were standing in front of it.

When the kids spilled into Josh's kitchen, they had runny noses and pink cheeks. They left their boots and jackets in the mudroom and walked into the kitchen in their socks.

Josh looked around the kitchen. He

didn't see Pal, but he did see a note on the table. It said: DAD AND I TOOK THE BOYS SLEDDING.—MOM

"Nate must be with them," Ruth Rose said. "He told my mom he was going sledding today."

"Okay, now let's check Pal's favorite sleeping places," Josh said.

They looked under all the tables, the couch, Josh's bed, and the twins' beds, but they couldn't find Pal. They didn't see a Valentine's card, either.

They checked the coat closet. Pal liked to snooze there on top of the sneakers.

They looked down the cellar stairs. Pal sometimes slept next to the furnace.

The kids called, "Pal, where ARE you?" No answer.

"Doesn't he have his own special bed?" Dink asked.

Josh laughed. "Yeah, I gave him an

old sweater of mine to sleep on," he said. "He drags it around the house like a toy."

Ruth Rose saw something sticking out from behind the sofa. "Is the sweater orange?" she asked Josh.

"Yup. That's why I gave it to Pal," Josh said. "It was *too* orange. When I put it on, I looked like a pumpkin!"

Ruth Rose looked behind the sofa. "Here he is," she said. Pal was lying on a bright orange sweater, snoring away.

When Josh got down on his knees, Pal opened his eyes. He licked Josh's fingers, then yawned.

Josh reached under the sweater. He pulled his hand out, holding a big red envelope. On the front, someone had written JOSH in gold glitter.

"We found it!" Josh said. He ripped open the envelope and removed the card. In the middle was a huge red heart

surrounded by little ones. The message read: HAY, JOSH, QUIT STALLING AND BE MY VALENTINE! FROM YOUR SEKRET ADMIRER.

"Two misspelled words," Ruth Rose said, reading over Josh's shoulder.

"I only see one," Dink said. "*Sekret,* like on my card."

"*Hay* is wrong," Ruth Rose said. "*Hay* is what cows eat. It should be spelled *H-E-Y,* like when you're calling someone."

Josh shook the envelope over the couch, and out fell a bunch of small letters and a two-inch piece of cardboard cut from a cereal box.

"Just like mine," Dink said. "This is getting interesting!"

Josh grabbed the cardboard. He read out loud: *"Where do jungle animals drink?"*

"Well, that one is easy," Dink said. "Jungle animals drink in the jungle."

"This must be a clue, like the other two about where Lincoln hangs out and where a buddy snores," Ruth Rose said. "Each clue asks *where*."

"Okay," Dink said. "Jungle animals drink in zoos, too."

"And they drink in cartoons on TV," Josh said.

"I'm betting it's closer to Green Lawn," Ruth Rose said. "Like the penny jar and the orange sweater. These secret admirers are around here!"

"But there are no jungle animals in Green Lawn," Dink said.

"I wish there were!" Josh said. "It would be cool to have elephants, monkeys, and lions walking down Main Street. People would totally freak out!"

"Not lions," Dink said. "Lions live on the African plains, not in the jungle."

"How about tigers?" Josh said. "Tigers prowl in the jungle."

Ruth Rose stared at Josh. "Yes, they do," she said. "And I just happen to have a cat named Tiger."

Both boys looked at Ruth Rose.

"Where does Tiger drink?" Josh asked her.

"She has a special bowl," Ruth Rose said. "It's in the pantry by the back door."

"Then I say we go look there," Dink said.

"Outside again?" Josh moaned. "But it's so nice and warm here!"

"Come on, Josh," Dink said. "Maybe your secret admirer has a big box of candy for you!"

"Okay, but let's look at my letters first," Josh said. He picked the letters off the couch and laid them end-to-end on the coffee table. The letters were *R, E, H, E,* and *W.*

Dink pulled out his own envelope

and dumped his letters next to Josh's. He put them in a long row. "So now we have *E, L, P, S, E, S, R, E, H, E,* and *W,*" he said.

"We could try to make words," Josh said.

"But maybe there'll be more letters," Ruth Rose said. "Let's wait until we have all of them."

"Good idea," Dink said. He dropped his letters back into his envelope, and Josh did the same with his five. They put the envelopes in their pockets.

Josh walked into the mudroom and got their stuff. "You're right, Ruth Rose," he said. "Plus, I have a feeling the next card we find is going to be for you!"

CHAPTER 5

Once again the kids trudged through the snow. They trekked down Farm Lane, kicking snow into the air.

"I wonder who these secret admirers are," Dink said.

"I think it's just one," Ruth Rose said.

"Why?" Dink asked.

"Because of *secret* spelled wrong," she said. "Most people know how to spell *secret*. I'll bet the same person made those cards, cut out the little letters, and wrote those clues!"

"The secret admirer is probably

some scientist who wants to study my incredible brain!" Josh said.

"Ha!" Dink barked. "Your incredible brain must be frozen. I think the secret admirer knows us. He knew about my penny jar and your sweater."

"And maybe Ruth Rose's cat," Josh added.

"We don't know for sure if Tiger is the real clue," Ruth Rose said. "Remember, we were wrong about my brother's giraffe."

"Hey, don't giraffes live in the jungle, too?" Josh asked.

"Nope," Dink said. "They hang out on the plains with the lions."

Josh tossed some snow at Dink. "How come you're so smart?"

Dink lobbed a snowball at Josh. "*My* incredible brain," he said.

Ruth Rose opened her back door. "Take your boots off," she told Dink and

Josh. "WE'RE HOME, MOM!"

No one answered. The kids kicked off their boots and hung up their jackets.

"This place is quiet," Josh said.

"There's a note, Ruth Rose," Dink said, pointing to the bulletin board next to the pantry.

OUT FOOD SHOPPING. HAVE A SNACK. WILL BE HOME SOON.—MOM

"Who goes food shopping in a blizzard?" Josh asked.

"Where's Tiger's dish?" Dink asked.

Ruth Rose pointed toward the pantry. "In there," she said. She walked into the pantry, with Dink and Josh right behind her.

Ruth Rose's cat lay on a small blanket. Her eyes were closed, and she was purring. Her whiskers twitched, and her tummy moved up and down as she breathed.

"There's her bowl," Ruth Rose said.

Tiger opened her eyes when Ruth Rose moved the water dish. Under it was a square red envelope.

"You got a card!" Josh said.

The three kids sat at the table, and Ruth Rose ripped open the envelope. She pulled out a card and a piece of a cereal box top. Then she spilled out five small pieces of paper that had been cut from a comic book.

Dink picked up the piece of cardboard. "Listen, here's the next clue," he said. *"Where do pigeons fly in and out?"*

"That's easy," Josh said. "Pigeons fly anywhere they want to!"

Ruth Rose looked at her Valentine's card. On the front were a big smiley face and her name, all written in glitter.

She opened the card and showed Dink and Josh what was written inside. It read: RUTH ROSE, I'M NOT LION. I WANT TO BE YOUR VALENTION. FROM YOUR SEKRET ADMIRER.

Josh grinned. "It's a poem," he said.

"*Lion* should be *lying,* right?" Dink said. "And *valentine* is spelled wrong, too."

"They wrote *valention* so it rhymes with *lion,*" Ruth Rose said.

"Right, and *secret* is spelled with a *K* again, just like in the other cards," Dink said.

"Let's look at my little letters," Ruth Rose said. They had landed on the table near a plate covered with a blue napkin.

"All this thinking is making me hungry," Josh said. He put his hand to his forehead, as if he were going to faint.

Ruth Rose removed the napkin. The plate was stacked with cookies. "Go ahead," she told Josh. "Mom left them here for us, anyway."

While Josh munched a cookie, Ruth Rose arranged the five letters in a row on the table: *L, Y, L, P, O.*

"This is crazy," Dink said, trying to make sense of the letters.

Josh moved some of the letters with his other hand. He read, "*Y, O, P, L, L,*" spitting cookie crumbs onto the table.

"Very nice table manners, Josh," Dink teased.

Ruth Rose sighed. "I'll bet there are more cards and clues and letters," she said. She scooped up her five letters and stuck them back in the envelope with the cardboard and her secret admirer card, and she put it all in her pocket.

The kids ate cookies and thought about the pigeon clue.

Ruth Rose gave Tiger a morsel, which the cat lapped out of her hand. Everyone at the table could hear Tiger's purring.

"Pigeons fly in the sky," Josh said. "Hey, I made a poem!"

"They fly to telephone wires," Dink said.

"Well, we probably won't find a clue in the sky," Ruth Rose said. She glanced toward the window. "Only billions of snowflakes."

"I sure hope our secret admirer didn't put a note up on some telephone pole or electric wires," Josh said.

The kids sat and thought. Josh took another cookie. "What if our admirer isn't talking about wild pigeons?" he asked. "What if he means tame pigeons, like pets?"

"Yeah, like those pigeons that people train," Dink said.

"They're called messenger pigeons or carrier pigeons," Ruth Rose said. "They can carry messages to people."

"How do you know this stuff?" Josh asked.

"My grandfather told me," Ruth Rose said. "In the First and Second World Wars, people would tie a tiny tube to a messenger pigeon's leg. They had put a message inside the tube, and the pigeon would fly it to where someone was waiting for the message. That person would take it out of the tube, then put in another message, and the pigeon would return to its coop."

"Why not just send a letter?" Dink asked. "Or call the other person on the telephone?"

Ruth Rose nodded. "I asked my grandfather that," she said. "He told me it was because in the wars, the mail either didn't get through or took too long to get there. And enemies could listen in on phone calls. So they used these pigeons."

"Boy, that's way cooler than email!" Josh said.

"So wild pigeons fly anywhere they want to, and tame pigeons fly in and out of pigeon coops," Dink offered after a minute. He looked out the window. "But I wonder if they do it in the snow."

"We don't know anyone who owns pigeons or coops," Josh said.

"Yes, we do! Mrs. Wong has pigeons," Ruth Rose said. "She sells them at Furry Feet. I saw a few there last week."

"You're a genius!" Josh told Ruth Rose. "Whoever she sells them to must have a coop. Maybe that's what this clue is trying to tell us. Let's go see Mrs. Wong!"

CHAPTER 6

The kids bundled up for the cold and headed back outside. They turned west on Woody Street, then hiked around the elementary school.

"Do you think Furry Feet is open on Sundays?" Josh said.

"I'll bet it's open today," Ruth Rose said. "Some people like to buy cute animals as Valentine's Day presents."

Not only was Furry Feet open, but a lot of people were inside, shopping and looking at the animals and fish.

Dink, Josh, and Ruth Rose saw

Mrs. Wong's nephew, Leonard. He was helping a boy and girl choose a goldfish. They were standing in front of a tank filled with fish.

"I like the black one with the bulgy eyes," the boy said. "It looks like a space alien!"

"And I like the orange one with the fluffy tail," his sister said. "It looks like a mermaid."

"Why don't you take both fish?" Leonard asked. "That way, they wouldn't be lonely. They'd be pals, like you guys are."

Their parents let the kids buy both fish. The kids left the store happy, already choosing names for their new pets.

"Hi, Leonard," Josh said. "Is your aunt around?"

Leonard waved a big hand. "She's in the back room," he said. "I think she's counting bags of dog chow for her next order." He pulled a cell phone out of his pocket. "I'll text her you're here."

Ruth Rose looked around the shop. "Do you still have pigeons?" she asked.

"A few," he said, "over there next to the parakeets."

While Leonard texted, the kids crossed the shop. They saw cages of canaries, parakeets, and lovebirds. They were all twittering and flapping their wings.

They stopped in front of the pigeon cage. The birds were making soft cooing noises.

"I should get a pigeon," Josh said. "I could train him to clean my room. He could eat the cookie crumbs off my bed!"

"These are homing pigeons," Ruth Rose said, reading the small sign attached to the cage front. "It says here you can train them to fly away and then come back home to their nest."

"Like the ones your grandfather told you about," Dink said.

There were three pigeons in the cage. One was white, one was dark gray, and the third was brown with white tips on its wing feathers. All three had round red eyes and pinky-red feet.

"These are so cool!" Josh said. "If we each bought one, we could send messages to each other!"

"You have to train them to do that," Ruth Rose said. "My grandpa said they can fly more than forty miles an hour!"

Mrs. Wong walked up behind the kids. "You're right, Ruth Rose," she said. "Some people race these pigeons, and they have been known to fly more than a thousand miles back to their coops!"

"How long does it take to train them to carry messages to people?" Josh asked.

"Gosh, I don't really know," Mrs.

Wong said. "Why, are you tired of cell phones and email?"

"We're following clues to solve a Valentine's Day mystery," Dink said.

Ruth Rose showed Mrs. Wong the Valentine's Day card and the cardboard that said WHERE DO PIGEONS FLY IN AND OUT?

"From your sekret admirer," Mrs. Wong read. "What fun! But whoever wrote this misspelled a word." She grinned. "Find a person who doesn't know how to spell very well, and you'll know who your secret admirer is, Ruth Rose."

Ruth Rose blushed.

"We figured you might know someone who keeps pigeons as pets," Dink said. "Pigeons fly in and out of coops, right?"

"Yes, they do," Mrs. Wong said. "My uncle in China had dozens of pigeons living in coops he built on the top of his house. The pigeons flew in and out all day long!"

"In China?" Josh said. "Do you know anyone here, in Green Lawn?"

"Let me think," Mrs. Wong said. "Most people buy these little beauties to keep in cages. They don't train them to fly in and out, as it says in your note."

Then Mrs. Wong snapped her fingers. "Oh, I *do* know someone who used to have homing pigeons!" she said. "Mr. and Mrs. Spivets had a coop in the Shangri-la Hotel attic! They bought some pigeons from me a few years back."

"We know them, sort of," Dink said. "They're Mr. Linkletter's aunt and uncle."

"Right, and they own the Shangri-la Hotel," Ruth Rose said.

Mrs. Wong nodded. "Mr. Spivets built a coop up there some years ago," she said. "I think he had a cousin in Vermont who also had pigeons, and they'd send each other notes."

"Do you think Mr. Spivets still has his pigeons?" Ruth Rose asked.

"He might," Mrs. Wong said. "Some pigeons live twenty years or more!"

CHAPTER 7

The kids headed down Main Street toward the Shangri-la Hotel. Snowflakes covered their hats and shoulders. The Green Lawn Savings Bank had a red heart in the window. A message read: TO ALL OUR CUSTOMERS, A BIG VALENTINE'S DAY THANK-YOU!

The kids reached the hotel and shoved open the thick glass door. Inside, it was warm and smelled good.

A fire crackled in the fireplace. In front of it, a man and woman sat reading. They each held a cup of tea. A plate of cookies sat on the table between their chairs.

Josh sniffed the air, the way Pal did when he was hungry.

"Peanut butter cookies!" Josh whispered. "My favorite food in the world!"

"Josh, you just had cookies at my house!" Ruth Rose said.

"But that was a half hour ago," Josh said, putting his hand to his forehead again. "Do you want me to starve?"

"Quit faking," Dink told his friend.

They walked up to the counter, where Mr. Linkletter stood watching them. He was a tall man with a thin mustache. His eyes looked sad, but the kids knew he was happy inside.

"Young people," Mr. Linkletter said. "What brings you out on such a snowy Sunday?"

They told him about the notes and cards they'd been finding. "We want to figure out who our secret admirer is!" Ruth Rose said.

"The last note asked where pigeons fly in and out," Josh said.

"So we went to Mrs. Wong, and she told us your aunt and uncle used to have pigeons," Ruth Rose added.

"So we came to see them!" Dink said.

Mr. Linkletter shook his head. "There are no more pigeons, and my aunt and uncle are in Florida on vacation." He looked at a small calendar on his desk. "They'll be back on Tuesday."

"But is the coop still up there?" Dink asked.

Mr. Linkletter looked toward the ceiling, as if he could see through it, all the way to the roof. "I believe so," he said. "But the pigeons stopped coming back some years ago."

"Could we see the coop, though?" Dink asked. "Because the note said *where* do pigeons fly in and out, and they flew in and out of the coop, right?"

Mr. Linkletter sighed. He picked up his desk calendar and gave it a quick polish with his sleeve. He straightened his tie and looked around the quiet lobby. Finally, he said, "I'll take you up."

He put out a small sign that said BACK IN FIVE MINUTES and motioned for the kids to follow him. They crowded into the elevator, and Mr. Linkletter pushed a button that took them to the top floor.

The elevator car opened into a dark, dusty hallway. There were no guest rooms, just some old furniture and cobwebs. It was cold, and Dink shivered.

Halfway down the hallway, Mr. Linkletter stopped and opened a door. He pointed up. "At the top of these stairs, you'll find another door," he said. "That door lets you into the attic. I believe the coop is next to the windows on the south wall."

Josh peeked up the stairs. "It's pretty dark up there," he said. He looked hopefully at Mr. Linkletter. "Are you coming with us?"

"No, sir," Mr. Linkletter said. "I don't want to get my suit dirty, and, well, I don't like spiders."

"You're afraid of spiders?" Josh asked.

"I am not *afraid* of spiders, young man," Mr. Linkletter said. "I just don't like all their creepy eyes and hairy legs."

"Well, we love dirty places and spiders!" Ruth Rose said. "Come on, guys, follow me!"

"Maybe *you* love spiders, Ruth Rose Hathaway," Josh mumbled under his breath. "But Josh Pinto doesn't!"

Ruth Rose scooted through the door

and began climbing the stairs. Josh gulped, then followed her. Dink was behind Josh. The stairs were so narrow that his shoulders brushed against the walls on both sides. He felt cobwebs on his face and hair. There was almost no light, just a little from the hallway below them.

Dink felt a cool draft on his face and hands, almost like a breeze. He smelled something unpleasant, like the cleaning stuff under the kitchen sink.

"There's about a million stairs!" Josh muttered.

"Keep going!" Dink said. "Your secret admirer is waiting to study your brain!"

"Very funny," Josh mumbled.

"I found the door!" Ruth Rose cried from the top of the stairs.

CHAPTER 8

By the time Dink and Josh reached her, Ruth Rose had shoved open a little door. They followed her into the attic, ducking low so they wouldn't bump their heads. Dim light came through two windows on the south wall. The windows were dirty and partly blocked with furniture.

Now Dink felt the cool breeze even more. One of the windows was open an inch at the bottom. Snowflakes had gathered on the floor, a little pile of white against the black.

"There better be a light up here,"

Josh said, "or I'm going back down!"

"Josh, don't be a—" Ruth Rose started to say.

Suddenly they all heard a deep voice. It was coming up the narrow, dark stairs they'd just climbed. *"Children,"* the voice said. *"Chiiiiillldren!"*

"Oh gosh, I knew this was a mistake," Josh moaned. "This hotel is about a zillion years old, and it's filled with ghosts!"

"Josh, last year we thought this place was haunted, remember?" Dink asked. "And we proved it isn't."

Josh shivered and pulled his coat collar up around his ears. "It still feels haunted to me!" he said.

Dink returned to the doorway and stuck his head through the opening. His heart was beating way too fast, even though he absolutely did not believe in ghosts.

"Children," the voice echoed, *"I have something for you. . . ."*

Dink gulped. He saw dark legs at the bottom of the steps. Then he noticed a glow around the legs. The feet moved slowly toward the stairs.

Dink could feel the tiny hairs on his arms stand up straight.

A familiar face looked up toward him. It was Mr. Linkletter, standing in the hallway. The glow came from a flashlight he was holding.

Mr. Linkletter aimed the flashlight up the stairs. "Dink, is that you?" he asked.

"Yup. I'll be right down!" Dink said. Now he felt silly thinking he'd seen a glowing ghost.

Dink scampered down the stairs.

"What's up there?" Mr. Linkletter whispered. "Any spiders?"

"I think so," Dink said. "Lots of cobwebs, anyway." He grinned. "Josh is scared practically out of his pants!"

Mr. Linkletter hardly ever smiled, but now his mustache twitched and his eyes crinkled. That was almost a smile.

"I thought you could use this," Mr. Linkletter said. He handed the flashlight to Dink.

"Thanks a lot," Dink said. "It'll make Josh feel better."

"I'll see you in the lobby," Mr. Linkletter said as he hurried down the hall.

Dink watched the tall, thin man disappear in the gloom. Then he climbed back up to the attic. "It was just Mr. Linkletter with this," Dink said, waving the flashlight.

Josh grabbed the light and shone it into his own face. "I knew it wasn't a ghost," he said. "I was just trying to scare you guys."

"Sure," Dink said. He made a goofy ghost face at Josh.

"The only one you scared was yourself," Ruth Rose said. She took the flashlight from Josh's hand and aimed its beam around the dim space. They were in an attic, all right. They saw a pile of mattresses, a few broken chairs, and a lot of old-timey stuff, all covered in thick dust.

A string hung over their heads. It was attached to an electric light cord. But the lightbulb socket was empty.

Ruth Rose turned the flashlight above their heads. Cobwebs dripped from the ceiling, clung to walls, and covered all the old abandoned furniture.

"If I see one creepy eye or hairy leg, I'm going to throw up," Josh said.

Dink giggled. "Don't let the spiders know you're afraid of them," he said. "If they hear you, they'll crawl up inside your pants and—"

"There's the coop!" Ruth Rose said.

She had aimed the flashlight toward
the south wall. What Dink had thought
was furniture in front of the windows
was a cage. It was about two feet square
and built of a wood frame covered in
wire screening.

"Mr. Linkletter and Mrs. Wong were
right!" Dink said. The kids walked closer.
The pigeon coop held small compart-
ments, where Dink could see old nests.

There were empty food and water dishes and old straw on the floor.

The coop stood on legs. Because it was positioned in front of the windows, the pigeons would have been able to fly from outside right into the coop.

On one side of the coop, there were small latched doors. Dink figured this was where the pigeons' owners could reach inside to get the pigeons or fill their dishes. But there were no pigeons now. Just a few feathers and pigeon waste.

Dink picked up a feather. When Josh turned away, Dink placed the feather on the back of his friend's neck. "Oh, Josh, there's a spider on you!" he whispered. "It has twelve creepy eyes and eight hairy legs!"

Josh jumped and whirled around in time to see Dink holding the feather. "Very mature, Dink," Josh said.

"This could be where pigeons fly

in and out," Ruth Rose said. "Like the clue said. Or they *used to* fly in and out, anyway."

"So let's look around for a red envelope," Josh said. "And then get out of here!"

"But how would anyone get up here to leave an envelope?" Dink asked.

"The same way we did," Josh said. "Just ask Mr. Linkletter."

"But wouldn't Mr. Linkletter have told us if anyone else came up here?" Dink asked.

Josh thought about that. "Maybe Mr. Linkletter is in on this whole secret admirer thing," he said. "If he's part of it, he wouldn't let us know if he brought anyone else up here."

Dink smiled, thinking about Mr. Linkletter's wiggly mustache and eyebrows. "You think Mr. Linkletter is our secret admirer?" he asked Josh. "You think he snuck into your house and hid a card under Pal's orange sweater?"

Josh smiled. "No, I doubt it," he said.

"Let's split up and look around for a red envelope," Ruth Rose suggested.

"Okay, but I get the flashlight!" Josh said, plucking it from Ruth Rose's fingers.

The kids looked in and under some old dressers. They undid the flaps on cardboard boxes and found old books and papers. They peeled back the mattresses and unrolled an old carpet. They even checked out each little pigeon compartment in the coop.

After twenty minutes of searching, all they had was cobwebs in their hair and dust all over their clothes and hands.

Josh sneezed. "When I get outside, I'm going to roll in the snow!" he said. He wiped his hands down the sides of his pant legs.

Dink was on his knees, opening another box. "Hey, look at this!" he said. Josh and Ruth Rose joined him. Josh shone the flashlight on the thin book Dink was holding. The front cover showed a brown-and-white pigeon flying into a coop.

"It's called *How to Train Homing Pigeons*," Dink said.

CHAPTER 9

Josh held the flashlight over the book as Dink opened to the first page. On the inside cover, someone had written: FOR EB SPIVETS, FROM HIS LOVING COUSIN, LUCAS SPIVETS.

Dink turned more pages. They saw pictures of pigeons flying into coops, flying out of coops, and nesting in coops like the one in front of the attic windows. In one picture, a mother pigeon was feeding two babies in a nest.

Josh swiped at a cobweb that was

tickling his cheek. When he moved his hand, the flashlight beam shone on something shiny on the bottom of the box.

Dink reached into the box and picked up three small silvery tubes. Each tube was about an inch long, and as thin as a pencil. The tubes had tiny caps so if you put something inside one of them, it couldn't fall out.

"What're those things?" Josh asked.

"Wait, I saw something like this in the book," Ruth Rose said. She flipped back a few pages. "There—that pigeon has one tied to its leg!"

She pointed to a drawing of a pigeon's leg and foot. Tied to the leg with a string was a tube like the ones Dink held in his hand.

"You're right. These are message tubes!" Dink said, reading the words under the picture. "It says you write a message, roll it up, and stick it in a tube.

Then the pigeon takes it to wherever it's supposed to go!"

"Like my grandfather told me," Ruth Rose said.

Dink opened all the little caps. Inside one tube he found a rolled-up piece of paper. He flattened it on his knee. The letters were faded, but written in beautiful handwriting: TO MY DEAR EB—HAPPY VALENTINE'S DAY. MY ANSWER IS YES! FROM YOUR SECRET ADMIRER. There was a date: FEBRUARY 14, 1950.

"Wow," Dink said. "This message was written on Valentine's Day sixty-five years ago!"

"At least *someone* can spell *secret*," Ruth Rose commented.

"So who's *My Dear Eb*?" Josh asked.

"I think Mr. Spivets's first name is Ebenezer," Dink said. "I'll bet this note is from his girlfriend back in 1950."

"That is so cool!" Josh said. "But why

didn't she just call him on the phone?"

"Josh, it was Valentine's Day," Ruth Rose said. "Maybe they thought having a pigeon deliver their messages was more romantic than making phone calls!"

Dink slipped the note into its tube and put the three tubes in his pocket. "I'll give them to Mr. Linkletter," he said. "I'll bet his uncle will be really happy to get this note back after sixty-five years!"

The kids finished looking through the book. On the back cover they saw a picture of a tall building in the snow, with trees showing over the roof. Pigeons were flying in through an open window.

"Yuck! Do pigeons live in people's houses?" Josh asked. "That would be smelly!"

"It's a barn," Dink said. "They're flying into a barn through that window where farmers used to load hay."

A sentence under the drawing said:
IN BAD WEATHER, SOME PIGEONS ROOST IN
GARAGES, BARNS, AND OTHER BUILDINGS.

"You're right," Ruth Rose said. "See, there's the top of the barn door, with those sliding things. Just like you have on your barn, Josh."

Josh stared at the picture. "Maybe that's what the note means!" he said. "We leave our barn door open sometimes so Polly gets fresh air. Pigeons go in all the time. You can hear them up on the beams!"

Dink glanced around the dim attic space. "We've been looking in the wrong place," he said. "Pigeons fly in and out of Josh's barn, not up here!"

"So we should go check it out," Ruth Rose said. "Maybe there's a card there for Josh."

Josh smiled. "You mean I have *two* secret admirers?" he asked.

"Lots of people like you," Ruth Rose told him.

"Don't tell him that!" Dink said.

"Come on, let's check out Josh's barn," Ruth Rose said.

Dink dropped the book back into the box. "Okay, let's go," he said.

The kids started backing down the steep, narrow stairs.

CHAPTER 10

Dink walked up to Mr. Linkletter, who was standing behind the counter.

"Did you find what you were looking for?" the hotel manager asked.

"We found the old coop," Josh said. "But no pigeons, just pigeon poop."

"Any—um—spiders?" Mr. Linkletter asked.

"Nope, just lots of cobwebs," Josh answered. "Oh, and Dink tried to scare me with a pigeon feather. But I just laughed."

"You laughed after you jumped ten feet in the air!" Dink said.

"We found something else," Ruth Rose said. "Show him, Dink."

Dink pulled the three silvery tubes from his pocket. He laid them on the counter.

"Oh, yes, I remember those," Mr. Linkletter said. "My uncle and his cousin Lucas used to send messages back and forth. They'd tuck notes inside these tubes and send a pigeon on its way."

Dink pulled the old note from its tube. "Look what else we found," he said. He unrolled the paper and handed it to Mr. Linkletter.

The tall man read the note, holding it carefully by its edges. "My stars," he said. "This is from my aunt Flo to Uncle Eb the year they were married!"

"Did your aunt have pigeons, too?" asked Ruth Rose.

"No, but her father did," Mr. Linkletter said. "Flo's father and my uncle Eb began exchanging notes, and one day Uncle Eb met Aunt Flo. Then *they* began sending notes, using the pigeons." Mr. Linkletter almost smiled. "And that turned into love."

"What does the note mean, *My answer is yes?*" Ruth Rose asked.

"I'm guessing Uncle Eb sent a note to Flo asking her to marry him," Mr. Linkletter said. "She must have returned this note with her answer. They were married two months later, in April 1950."

"Did you go to the wedding?" Josh asked.

"Goodness no!" Mr. Linkletter said. "That was over sixty-five years ago, and I wasn't even born!"

"Would your aunt and uncle like to have these tubes and the note?" Dink asked.

"I'm sure they will be thrilled," Mr.

Linkletter said. He slid the tubes into an envelope and put it in a drawer under the counter. "I'll make sure they get them."

The kids said good-bye to Mr. Linkletter and walked outside. The snow had stopped, but it was still cold.

Dink looked toward the clock on the town hall. "It's almost three o'clock," he said. "We've been following clues all day, and we still don't know who our secret admirer is!"

"Let's hope we find something at my barn," Josh said. "Otherwise, we have to find some *other* place where pigeons fly in and out."

Dink, Josh, and Ruth Rose took the shortest route to Josh's house. They hiked across the town tennis courts, cut through the high school playing fields, and crossed Woody Street to Farm Lane.

"Let's go in and make some hot chocolate," Josh suggested as they passed his house.

"But don't you want to find the next clue?" Ruth Rose asked. "Where pigeons fly in and out?"

They all looked at the tall barn. Snow covered the roof and windowsills. Someone had shoveled a wide path from the house to the barn.

"I guess my dad got back from sledding," Josh said.

"Josh, what's that on the barn door?" Dink asked. "It's red!"

They raced across Josh's backyard, kicking snow out of their way.

Josh reached the door first. Someone had tied a red envelope to a nail. "I guess I *do* have two secret admirers!" Josh said.

Dink grinned. "Open the card."

Josh pulled the envelope from the

nail, opened it, and peeked inside.

"Why don't we go in your house to read it?" Dink asked. "My nose is freezing!"

The kids turned and ran to Josh's back door. They kicked their boots off, dropped their jackets, and sat at the kitchen table.

Josh pulled the Valentine's card from its envelope and put it on the table. Like Dink's, this card had glitter all over a big red heart. Josh opened the card. He read the message and started to laugh.

"What's it say?" Ruth Rose asked.

Josh read it out loud:

Noses are red,
berries are blue.
You helped me, and I love you!
      From your sekret admirer

"The same great speller," Josh said.

"Someone loves you," Dink said, grinning at his friend.

"Someone you helped," Ruth Rose said. "Who have you helped, Josh?"

CHAPTER 11

"I help a lot of people," Josh said. "I help my mom and dad. I help the twins with homework and stuff."

Dink grinned. "You help the twins with their homework?" he asked. "Or do they help you with yours?"

Josh looked at Dink. "Very funny," he said. "Oh, and I help you, Dink, by being your friend. Without me, you wouldn't have any friends at all!"

Dink laughed. "Gee, I thought it was the other way around," he said.

"Do you think someone in your family wrote this?" Ruth Rose tapped the card.

Josh shook his head. "Nope. My mom and dad know how to spell *secret,*" he said. "And the twins can't spell *admirer.* They probably don't even know what it means!"

"Someone else you helped, then," Dink said. "How about a neighbor?"

Josh laughed. "A neighbor wrote *I love you* in a card and hung it on my barn door?" he said. "I don't think so."

Ruth Rose tapped the envelope. "Let's look at what else is in there," she said.

Josh emptied the envelope onto the table. Four little squares of paper fell out. Josh arranged them so they could read the letters: *K, O, L, O.*

"There's no piece of cardboard?" Dink asked.

Josh peeked inside the envelope. "Nope. Just the card and these letters."

"So there's no new clue," Ruth Rose said.

"Good!" Josh said. "I'm tired of running all over town in the snow!"

"Yeah, me too," Dink said. "But we still don't know anything. We all have a secret admirer, but we don't know who it is."

"I have two," Josh said. He wiggled two fingers in front of Dink's face.

"Whatever," Dink answered.

"Let's go over the four clues," Ruth Rose suggested. "Dink, your first one asked where Abe Lincoln hangs out, right?"

Dink nodded. "I remembered he hangs out on pennies, and I found my card under my penny jug. The second clue asked where a buddy snores."

"So then we came here," Josh said,

"and I found a card with the third clue under Pal's sweater. The clue asked where jungle animals drink."

"Then we went to my house, and I found my card under Tiger's water dish," Ruth Rose added. "The fourth clue asked where pigeons fly in and out."

"Then we came to my barn," Josh said. "I got another envelope and card, but no new clue inside."

"But we do have your new letters," Ruth Rose said.

"And we still don't know what they mean," Josh said.

"Why don't we try to make words out of all of them?" Dink asked. "The secret admirer must have put the letters in the envelopes because they spell something, right?"

They emptied their pockets and laid all the letters on the table.

Dink arranged them into four rows with five letters in each row. "Twenty in all," he said. "How should we do this?"

"Well, there are four *E*'s," Ruth Rose said. "And four *L*'s." She moved the *E*'s and *L*'s into two separate piles.

"Three *O*'s, two *P*'s, and two *S*'s," Josh said, making more piles. "There are five letters left over: *R, H, W, Y,* and *K.*" He made a pile of the single letters.

Ruth Rose counted the *E*'s and the *O*'s. "Seven vowels, and all the rest are consonants," she said.

The kids stared at the little piles of

letters. "It's impossible," Dink said. "We could probably make a hundred different words out of these."

"What if we tried using the letters the way we found them?" Ruth Rose asked. "Dink, do you remember which letters were in your envelope?"

"Sure," he said, reaching for the piles. "My letters were two *E*'s, two *S*'s, an *L*, and a *P*." He pulled those letters away from the others.

"How about you, Josh?" Ruth Rose asked. "What letters were in the envelope you found under Pal's sweater?"

"Easy peasy," Josh said. He dragged *R, E, H, E,* and *W* and placed them in front of him at the table. "These were in my first envelope."

"Okay, and mine were *L, Y, L, P,* and *O*," Ruth Rose said. She arranged those letters in front of her on the table.

"And the ones we just found on the

barn door are *O, L, O,* and *K,*" Dink said. He pushed those letters in front of Josh.

Josh looked at Ruth Rose. "Now what?" he asked. "This is still alphabet soup!"

Dink laughed. "Josh is still hungry."

"I think our secret admirer put these letters in our envelopes so we'd make words," Ruth Rose said. "So let's try."

"Josh has two piles," Dink said. "He has to make two words."

"Right," Josh said. "Because I'm twice as smart!"

CHAPTER 12

Dink, Josh, and Ruth Rose moved their letters around, trying to create words.

"It's sort of like Scrabble," Josh muttered. He had two little piles of letters in front of him. "Hey, I made *kool*!" he cried.

Ruth Rose and Dink looked at Josh's word.

"That's not how you spell *cool*," Dink said.

"But we know that our secret admirer can't spell, either," Josh said.

"Keep trying," Ruth Rose said.

"You guys are no fun," Josh mumbled. He moved letters around. "How about *kloo?*"

"Nope," Dink said. "*Clue* is spelled *C-L-U-E.* But if you move the *K,* you get *look.* That's a real word!"

"Awesome," Josh said. "I'd call you brilliant, but I don't want you to get all proud of yourself."

"No problem," Dink said. He moved *P, E, S, E, L,* and *S* around quickly. "What if I put an *S* at the beginning and kept the other *S* at the end?"

He tried it, then said, "Is *speels* a word?"

Ruth Rose looked over. "I don't think so, but *sleeps* is!" she said. "Just switch the *P* and the *L.*"

"Thanks, Ruth Rose," Dink said. "It's easier when we help each other."

"Okay, then help me with my second word," Josh said. His letters were arranged to read *R, E, H, E,* and *W.*

"*Rehew* isn't a word," Dink said.

"I know that," Josh said.

"Try putting the *W* in front of the *H*," Ruth Rose suggested. "Like in *who, what, when . . .*"

Josh did, and then he yelled, "Hey, what about *where*?"

"I don't see any other possibilities," Dink said. "So now we have three words: *look, sleeps,* and *where.*"

"Remember, all the other clues started with the word *where,*" Ruth Rose said. "Maybe this is another clue starting the same way!"

"*Where look sleeps,*" Josh attempted. "Nope."

"*Where sleeps look,*" Dink said. "Double nope."

"We need your word," Josh told Ruth Rose.

"Okay, but help me," she said.

The boys looked at her letters: *L, Y, L, P, O.*

"Maybe the two *L*'s should go together," Dink said. "Like in *Sally, Billy, silly, Molly . . .*"

"*Polly!*" Ruth Rose screamed. "You *are* a genius, Dink!"

"Don't tell him that!" Josh said.

The kids put the four words together in a row. They looked down at the sentence they had created: *Look where Polly sleeps.*

"Polly, my pony?" Josh said. "She sleeps in her stall in the barn."

"Then that's where we should look next!" Ruth Rose said.

Dink looked out the window at the bright sun on the white snow. The barn's shadow covered half the yard. "You think our secret admirer is in a cold barn?" he asked.

"We won't know till we look," Ruth

Rose said. She was already pulling on her jacket. "So far, every time we followed a clue, we found something new."

Dink and Josh grabbed their jackets, and the three headed outside. They crossed the yard on the hard-packed snow.

"Look," Dink said, pointing at something on the ground. "Tire tracks. But there are no cars here."

"My dad must have been here," Josh said. "Because the driveway is shoveled. Maybe he went out again."

The barn door was closed, and the kids shoved it open. Inside, it was dark except for a little light coming through the small windows.

"Where's the light switch?" Ruth Rose asked.

"Next to the door," Josh said. He reached past Dink and flipped a switch. Nothing happened.

"Bulb must be out," Josh muttered.

"If you leave the door open, we can still see what's in Polly's stall," Dink said.

The kids walked down the center of the barn, toward the end. The barn had four horse stalls, but three of them were empty. Polly's was the fourth.

Above them, they could hear pigeons cooing and fluttering their wings.

Dink smelled the hay. Under their feet, the barn floorboards creaked.

They stopped in front of Polly's stall door. The pony reached her head out to give Josh a nuzzle.

"Hey, Polly," Josh said. "Do you have a clue for us?"

Suddenly the overhead lights went on. People came running out of the three empty stalls. They were laughing and yelling, "SURPRISE! HAPPY VALENTINE'S DAY! BE MY VALENTINE!"

CHAPTER 13

Dink, Josh, and Ruth Rose froze in their tracks. Polly rose up on her hind legs and whinnied. Pal ran around everyone, barking and wagging his tail.

"What's going on?" Josh said to his parents, who were hugging him. "You guys almost gave me a heart attack!"

Dink's parents were there, too. And Ruth Rose's. Her brother, Nate, ran out of a stall, followed by Brian and Bradley. The three boys tossed pink and red streamers all over the older kids.

"It's a party for you guys!" Brian yelled. "You said you never got anything on Valentine's Day!"

"How do you know I said that?" Josh asked. "You weren't there."

"But we were listening!" Bradley said. "You should keep your door closed, bro."

Suddenly Mrs. Wong appeared, then Mr. Linkletter. They each held plates of cupcakes and cookies. The other adults made tables out of hay bales and sheets of plywood. More food came out of the empty stalls. Pink heart-shaped cookies, tubs of ice cream, containers of hot chocolate.

"Are you our secret admirers?" Josh asked Mrs. Wong and Mr. Linkletter.

Mrs. Wong made a little bow. "No, but we were happy to play along," she said.

"We do admire you," Mr. Linkletter

added. "But we're not your secret admirers."

"Then who is?" asked Ruth Rose.

Ruth Rose's father reached behind him, then held out Tiger, wearing a red heart on her collar. "Tiger is *your* secret admirer!" he told Ruth Rose. "Because you brush her and make sure she has food and water every day."

Dink's mother opened her carryall and pulled out his guinea pig. Loretta was wearing a red heart around her furry neck. "Loretta is *your* secret admirer!" his mom told him. "She loves you because you talk to her and keep her cage clean."

"Hey, what about me?" Josh asked. "Who's my secret admirer?"

"Actually, you don't have one," his father said. Then he smiled. "You have *two*!"

He led Polly out of her stall. The pony

was wearing a red heart on her halter. "Polly loves you because you brush her and feed her and let her give you pony kisses!"

Just then Pal jumped up on Josh's knee and barked. Josh could see a red heart on his collar.

"Pal loves you most," Josh's mother said. "Because you rescued him when his owners went to jail. You brought him home, even when I didn't want a dog. Pal will never forget your kindness."

Josh laughed. "So our pets are our secret admirers?" he asked.

"Yes, your pets, who love you," his mom said.

Dink smiled, remembering the clues that he, Josh, and Ruth Rose had found. "Which one of our pets doesn't know how to spell *secret*?" he asked.

"You'll have to ask them," his father said with a big grin.

They all sat on bales of hay and ate pink cookies, ice cream, and cupcakes with red frosting.

The next Saturday, the sun came out. The snow started to melt. Icicles dripped outside Josh's bedroom window. He and Dink and Ruth Rose were playing Scrabble on the floor.

Next to Josh, Pal lay on his orange sweater, snoring. He was still wearing a red heart on his collar.

It was Dink's turn. He made the word *sekret.* "Eighteen points, please," he said.

"No way, blue jay," Josh said. *"Secret* is spelled with a *C."*

Dink laughed. "Who says?"

Just then they all heard horns tooting down in the driveway. Doors were slamming. People were laughing.

"What's going on?" Josh asked.

Ruth Rose got to the window first. "Mrs. Wong is here!" she said. "And Mr. Linkletter!"

Dink and Josh ran to the window. "Who are those other people?" Dink asked.

"Oh my gosh," Josh said. "I think that's Mr. and Mrs. Spivets!"

A kid on a bicycle rode into the driveway.

"It's Leonard, Mrs. Wong's nephew!" Dink said.

"Come on!" Josh cried. They all clamored down the stairs and ran outside, tugging on their jackets.

Josh's parents were in the yard, too, chatting with the others. Brian and Bradley were standing next to Mrs. Wong's car, peeking in the windows.

"Hey, Dad, what's going on?" Josh asked.

All the grown-ups looked at Dink, Josh, and Ruth Rose. Mr. Linkletter stepped forward, holding Mr. and Mrs. Spivets's hands.

"My aunt and uncle have something to say to you three," Mr. Linkletter said.

CHAPTER 14

Mrs. Spivets had white hair and pink cheeks. She wore a blue sweater decorated with big white snowflakes. Her hat and mittens matched the sweater. She smiled at the three kids.

"Hello, dears," she said. "I am over eighty, and I have never received such a thoughtful gift. Thank you!"

She showed them a silver chain around her neck. Dangling from the chain was a silver tube. "I was so thrilled to see my note to Eb, which you discovered up in that horrid attic! Now I can keep it with this one."

Mrs. Spivets opened the little tube and pulled out a small piece of paper. She handed it to Ruth Rose. "Read it, my dear."

Ruth Rose read: *"My darling Flo, make me the happiest man in the world and marry me. Your secret admirer."*

Mr. Spivets cleared his throat. "I wrote that note when I was twenty!" he said. "And my dear wife kept it all these years."

"My sweet Ebenezer asked me to marry him on Valentine's Day 1950," Mrs. Spivets said. "I sent him my answer by pigeon, but it got lost until you sweethearts found it!"

Mrs. Spivets turned to her husband. "Give them their gift, dear," she said.

Mr. Spivets handed Dink a small package, wrapped in red tissue. Dink passed it to Josh. "He likes to open presents," Dink explained.

Josh pulled the wrapping paper off. Inside was the book they'd seen in the hotel attic: *How to Train Homing Pigeons.*

"Cool!" Josh said. "But, um, well, we don't have any pigeons."

"Yes, you do!" said Mrs. Wong. She opened the rear door of her car. Leonard reached in and pulled out a small wire cage. Inside were the three pigeons from Furry Feet.

"One for each of you!" Leonard said.

"Thank you!" Ruth Rose said.

"Awesome!" Josh said.

"This is so amazing!" Dink said.

"They'll need a place to sleep," Mr. Linkletter said. He walked over to his big old station wagon and opened the back. Inside was the pigeon coop from the Shangri-la attic. It had been cleaned and painted. Fresh straw lined the floor. Clean dishes for water and food were attached to the side.

"This is the best Valentine's present I ever got!" Josh said. "Even better than red cupcakes!"

Josh's father and Leonard wrestled the coop out of the station wagon. "Where do you think we should put it?" Josh's dad asked.

"Up in the barn!" Josh said.

Everyone walked to the barn. Leonard carried the coop. Mrs. Wong carried the pigeons. Mr. Spivets held his wife's hand.

Dink, Josh, and Ruth Rose were still standing in the driveway.

"We got pigeons!" Josh said. "I can't wait to train mine to deliver notes."

"I'm naming mine Flo, for Mrs. Spivets," Ruth Rose said.

"I'm calling mine Eb, for her husband," Dink said.

Josh didn't say anything.

"Josh, what are you going to name your pigeon?" Ruth Rose asked.

"I've thought of two names," Josh said. "But I'm having a hard time choosing between them."

"Between what and what?" Dink asked.

Josh raced toward the barn. "Between Dink and Ruth Rose!" he shouted over his shoulder.

DID YOU FIND THE
SECRET MESSAGE
HIDDEN IN THIS BOOK?

If you don't want
to know the answer,
don't look at the bottom
of this page!

. . . solve
mysteries
from A to Z!

Here's what kids, parents, and teachers have to say to Ron Roy about the **A TO Z MYSTERIES**® series:

"Whenever I go to the library, I always get an A to Z Mystery. It doesn't matter if I have read it a hundred times. I never get tired of reading them!" —Kristen M.

"I really love your books!!! So keep writing and I'll keep reading." —Eddie L.

"Keep writing fast or I will catch up with you!" —Ryan V.

"I love your books. You have quite a talent to write A to Z Mysteries. I like to think I am Dink. RON ROY ROCKS!" —Patrick P.

"Nothing can tear me away from your books!" —Rachel O.

"I like Dink the best because he never gives up, and he keeps going till he solves the mystery." —Matthew R.

"Sometimes I don't even know my mom is talking to me when I am reading one of your stories." —Julianna W.

"Your books are famous to me."
—Logan W.

"I think if you're not that busy, you could do every letter again." —Abigail D.

"I credit your books as one of the main influences that turned [my daughter] from a listener to a voracious reader."
—Andrew C.

"You have changed my third grader from an 'I'll read it if it is easy' boy into a 'let's go to the library' boy. Thank you so much, and please, keep up the great work."
—Kathy B.

"My third-grade students are now hooked on A to Z Mysteries! Thank you for sharing your talents with children and helping to instill in them a love for reading."
—Carolyn R.

A to Z Mysteries® fans, check out Ron Roy's other great mystery series!

Capital Mysteries

#1: Who Cloned the President?
#2: Kidnapped at the Capital
#3: The Skeleton in the Smithsonian
#4: A Spy in the White House
#5: Who Broke Lincoln's Thumb?
#6: Fireworks at the FBI
#7: Trouble at the Treasury
#8: Mystery at the Washington Monument
#9: A Thief at the National Zoo
#10: The Election-Day Disaster
#11: The Secret at Jefferson's Mansion
#12: The Ghost at Camp David
#13: Trapped on the D.C. Train!
#14: Turkey Trouble on the National Mall

Calendar Mysteries

January Joker
February Friend
March Mischief
April Adventure
May Magic
June Jam
July Jitters
August Acrobat
September Sneakers
October Ogre
November Night
December Dog
New Year's Eve Thieves

If Josh makes you laugh, meet another funny redhead!

MARVIN REDPOST

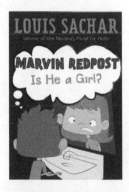

If you like **A to Z Mysteries**®, take a swing at

BALLPARK®
Mysteries

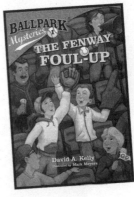